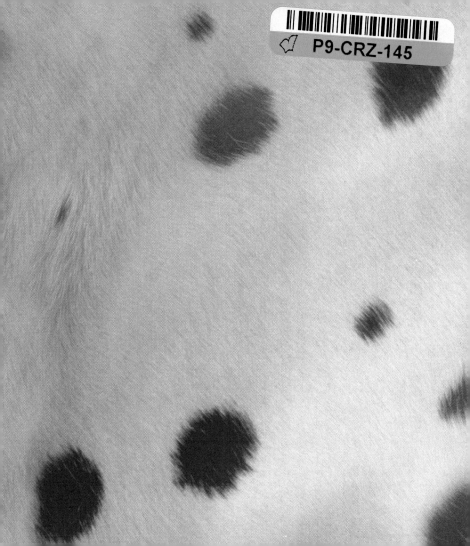

Creative Director   **Susie Garland Rice**
Art Direction   **Shannon Osborne Thompson**

10750a/The Emperor's New Clothes

There once was an Emperor who loved clothes. Every day he wasted hours putting on clothes for all occasions: robes for breakfast, shirts for tea, pants to go walking, and coats made especially for important dinners. He spent more time thinking about his clothes than being a good ruler.

The Emperor's New Clothes

A Hans Christian Andersen story

Retold by John Duncan

Illustrated by Danny Brooks Dalby

Dalmatian Press

Before long the Emperor heard about the amazing cloth. He thought, "If I had clothes made of this cloth, I would be able to tell right away who the most trustworthy subjects in my kingdom were."

The Emperor sent word to the tailors to make him a suit from this special cloth. The tailors told the Emperor that they needed a large bag of gold to purchase their magical threads.

They snickered because their plan was in action.

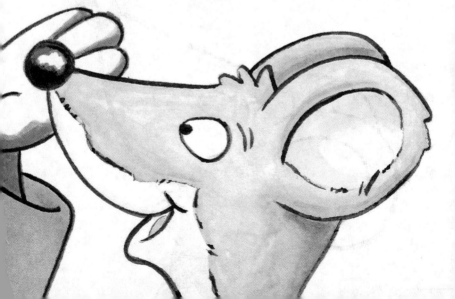

The Emperor sent the gold right away, and the tailors set to work at once. They pretended to cut, sew, and stitch, even though the spinning looms were empty. They even pulled imaginary threads through needles! Each day they requested another bag of gold and continued pretending to work.

The Emperor was anxious to see his unique new suit. But he became concerned about seeing the clothes for the first time. What if he couldn't see them? Surely they wouldn't be invisible to him! Just to be safe, though, he sent his assistant to inspect the work.

The tailors pretended to hold up beautiful samples of the fabric. The Emperor's assistant looked and looked, but he couldn't see anything. Even though he knew he was trustworthy and loyal, he worried that he might lose his job if anyone knew he couldn't see the cloth. So he said, "What a splendid pattern — and such charming colors!"

The tailors told the Emperor's assistant they needed more gold to buy more magical thread to complete the suit. The assistant returned to the Emperor and told him how wonderful the suit would be when it was finished, but that the tailors needed more gold to buy more thread. Excited and curious, the Emperor sent another assistant to see the suit and to take more gold.

This assistant, too, couldn't see a single stitch. The tailors pointed to various patterns and shapes in the cloth that wasn't there. The assistant thought to himself, "The Emperor will think I am unfit to serve if I tell him I didn't see anything." So he complimented the tailors on their work and reported to the Emperor that the cloth was the most amazing he had ever seen.

Everyone in the city heard about the beautiful new clothes. At last it was time for the Emperor to see for himself. He entered the shop as the tailors snipped away with scissors in the air.

"Isn't it lovely?" they asked, holding up imaginary pants, a shirt, and a cape. The Emperor was speechless. He couldn't see anything at all!

The Emperor thought to himself, "I'm the most honest of all — why can't I see?" Even though he saw nothing, he exclaimed, "Magnificent! Splendid! I will wear this suit in the grand procession tomorrow!" The tailors laughed and laughed after the Emperor left, thinking about how they would spend all their gold.

The next morning the Emperor was ready to dress in his new clothes. His helpers pretended to hand him pants, a shirt, and a cape. "How splendid you look, Your Majesty," remarked his court, even though he had on no clothes at all! As the grand procession began, the attendants pretended to carry the train of the Emperor's invisible cape as he marched in front of all the people in the city.

The crowd cheered, "Bravo! Beautiful! Hooray!" Then a little boy in the crowd cried out, "But the Emperor has on nothing at all... Look! Look!" The Emperor realized that the little boy was the most honest of all, and that even the Emperor had some lessons to learn.

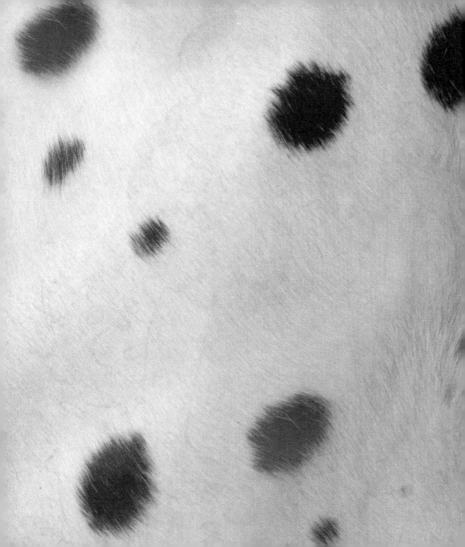